Rufus Goes to Sea

by
Kim T. Griswell

illustrated by
Valeri Gorbachev

STERLING CHILDREN'S BOOKS
New York

Rufus Leroy Williams III loved going to school.

He loved reading.

He loved writing.

He loved playtime and naptime and storytime.

But one day, Rufus found the school door locked.

SUMMER CAMP!
HERE WE COME!

SCHOOL BUS

Rufus sat down to read his favorite book.

Rufus read about days of adventure.

He read about nights under blankets of stars.

Rufus knew just what to do for summer vacation.

He would become a pirate.

Rufus packed his lunchbox, put on his backpack,
and picked up his blanket. Then he called a taxi.

"My name is Rufus Leroy Williams III,"
said Rufus, "and I want to be a pirate."

"Hang on!" said the taxi driver.

Rufus Leroy Williams III trotted to the ship.

He looked up, up, up at the deck. Then he opened his book.

"Permission to come aboard!"

Pyrate Wnted!

"Permission to come aboard!" shouted Rufus.

"Shiver me whiskers!" said First Mate Scratchwhiskers. "It's a pig!"

Faces peered over the rail.

"My name is Rufus Leroy Williams III," said Rufus, "and I want to be a pirate."

"Arrrh! No pigs on pirate ships!" growled Captain Wibblyshins.

"Why not?" asked Rufus.

SCURVY DOG

"Because pigs play on the poop deck," said the captain.

"They swing from the yardarm."

"They picnic in the crow's nest."

"And they wipe their chins with the Jolly Roger."

Rufus frowned. "But I have a backpack, a lunchbox, and a blanket!" he said.

"Arrrh! Useful gear," said Captain Wibblyshins. "But not what the pirate I be lookin' fer needs." And he waved Rufus on his way.

Rufus Leroy Williams III really wanted to be a pirate. And he knew just what he needed.

Rufus scurried aboard the *Scurvy Dog*. He grabbed a mop and went to work.

"Pig on the quarter deck!" called First Mate Scratchwhiskers. "And he has a hat."

Captain Wibblyshins clumped down the steps. "No pigs on a pirate ship," he said.

"Why not?" asked Rufus.

"Because pigs tangle up the ratlines," said the captain.

"They roll up in the hammocks."

"Pigs draw on the treasure maps and build castles with the pirate's booty."

"Not me!" Rufus held up the mop
and pointed to the deck.

"Arrrh! We already have a deck-swabbin' pirate,"
said Captain Wibblyshins. "The pirate I be lookin' fer needs
a different skill." And he shooed Rufus off the ship.

Rufus Leroy Williams III really, really wanted to be a pirate. And he knew just what he needed.

"Nice eye patch," said the ship's cook.
"But we already have a potato-peelin' pirate."
And he shooed Rufus out of the galley.

Rufus Leroy Williams III knocked on the captain's door.
"Permission to speak, Captain!" said Rufus.

The captain sat up in his bunk. "No one interrupts
the captain's nap!" he roared.

"But you need a pirate!" said Rufus.
"And I have a hat and an eye patch."

"Useful gear," said Captain Wibblyshins. "But the pirate I be lookin' fer needs somethin' else." And he marched Rufus to the plank.

"Wait!" Rufus wobbled back to the deck.
He held up his book. "I have this!"

Captain Wibblyshins wiggled his eyebrows.
"Can ye read it?"

"Yes!" said Rufus.

"Why didn't ye say so? A readin' pirate is just what we need!"

Captain Wibblyshins handed Rufus a treasure map. "Show us what yer made of, piglet!"

Rufus Leroy Williams III unrolled the map.

"Sail into the full moon.
Turn right at sunrise.
Stop when you hit dry land.
Dig where X marks the spot."

"Welcome to the crew!"
said Captain Wibblyshins.
"Mr. Scratchwhiskers!
Hoist the sails!"

Rufus loved being a pirate.

He loved rolling seas.

He loved salty breezes.

And he loved teaching the pirates their A, B, Cs (especially the letter P).

But he loved finding buried
treasure most of all . . .

. . . because new adventures waited inside.